This Book Donated By

Kayla Mayes
February 10, 1999

The Birthday Book Club

Presented
2-20-2008

©Highsmith® Inc. 1999

The Next-Door Dogs

The Next-Door Dogs

Colby Rodowsky

Pictures by Amy June Bates

FARRAR STRAUS GIROUX
NEW YORK

To Robbie

Text copyright © 2005 by Colby Rodowsky
Illustrations copyright © 2005 by Amy June Bates
Distributed in Canada by Douglas & McIntyre Publishing Group
Printed in the United States of America
Designed by Jay Colvin
First edition, 2005
3   5   7   9   10   8   6   4

www.fsgkidsbooks.com

Library of Congress Cataloging-in-Publication Data
Rodowsky, Colby F.
    The next-door dogs / Colby Rodowsky ; pictures by Amy
June Bates.— 1st ed.
        p.   cm.
    Summary: Although terrified of dogs, nine-year-old Sara forces
herself to face a Labrador retriever and a Dalmatian when she
must help her next-door neighbor, who has fallen and broken
her leg.
    ISBN-13: 978-0-374-36410-6
    ISBN-10: 0-374-36410-9
    [1. Dogs—Fiction.   2. Fear—Fiction.   3. Courage—Fiction.
4. Neighborliness—Fiction.]   I. Bates, Amy June, ill.   II. Title.

PZ7.R6185Ne 2005
[Fic]—dc22

                                                        2004043333

Contents

The Next-Door Dogs

Who, Me?

"**T**hey have cookies at the market with twisty chocolate tops," said Sara.

"Or giant soft pretzels," said Jessica.

"Or," said Cindy, "maybe we'll go to the drugstore and get one of those really big bags of M&M's on account of that's my mother's most favorite candy of all."

Sara and her friends were heading for the neighborhood shopping center one afternoon so that Cindy could buy a birthday present for her mother. They zigzagged along the sidewalk on Deepdene Road, carefully hopping over cracks. They crossed the alley and went past the pet store and the children's bookstore and the gift shop with the funny name. It was called Bungees.

"Wait!" said Cindy, catching hold of her friends and pulling them back to stand in front of the plate-glass window, which was filled with bowls and aprons and candlesticks. "Let's go in *there*."

"To Bungees?" said Sara. "Things in there will cost way more than you can spend."

"Let's go anyway," said Cindy. "Maybe

they'll have something super-small that won't be very much money."

Jessica held the door open, and a cool, spicy apple smell greeted them. The girls made their way to the back of the shop. They stopped to pick up coasters and china boxes and a tiny mirror with flowers painted on the edges, first looking at the prices, then setting the objects carefully back on the shelves.

Sara followed Cindy and Jessica for a while, until she spotted a large red-and-blue-and-yellow platter in the form of a fish. As she stood looking at it, she began to imagine what it would be like if there were dishes made like all the foods people ate. She thought about platters shaped like chickens and T-bone steaks and even waffles. She had just begun to picture a serving bowl that was like a sweet potato, sort of lumpy and pointy on the ends, the way sweet potatoes are, when she spotted a *very large* something coming around a display of umbrellas.

It was a dog. A *very large* black and shiny dog with tags on its collar that jangled as it walked. And it was coming right toward Sara.

That quickly, Sara stopped thinking about fish platters and sweet-potato bowls. That quickly, she headed away from the dog and scooted around a counter piled with place mats and picture frames. That quickly, she was out on the sidewalk in front of the store.

Sara moved down the block and stared into the bookstore window while she waited for her friends. She wiped her hands down the sides of her jeans and took slow, deep breaths, sure that everyone walking by could hear her heart going thumpa thumpa thumpa.

"What happened to you?" asked Jessica, when she and Cindy came out of the shop. "One minute you were there, and then Buster, the owner's dog, came along, and suddenly you weren't."

"Yeah," said Cindy, rolling her eyes. "If I didn't know better, I'd think you were afraid of dogs."

"Who, me?" screeched Sara. "No way. I'm not afraid of *anything*."

More about Sara

But Sara Barker was afraid of dogs. She was nine years old and was pretty sure that she was too old to be afraid. But she was anyway. She was afraid of the ruffing noise they made when they barked and the way they sometimes showed their big white pointed teeth. She was even afraid of the way they swoosh—swoosh—swooshed their tails back and forth.

Most of the time, Sara thought of herself as a *very brave person*. She didn't mind thunderstorms or snakes or slithery, slimy worms. She liked scary movies, lions in the zoo, and haunted houses at Halloween.

But dogs were a different story.

The worst thing about being afraid of dogs, aside from the shivery feeling Sara got whenever she saw one, was trying to keep other people from finding out.

Except for her family, of course. Sara's mother and father knew, and so did her twelve-year-old brother, Will, and her grandparents and aunts and uncles.

Mrs. Barker had long talks with Sara,

mostly at bedtime, about her fear and what she could do to overcome it. She even once took Sara to visit a friend whose dog had just had a litter of puppies. Sara had stood looking down at the mother dog surrounded by six little balls of white fur. But as she watched them, the palms of her hands began to sweat and her stomach felt twitchy. She ran outside and waited on the porch until her mother was ready to go.

Mr. Barker brought books home for Sara that were all about dogs: big ones and little ones; dogs in circuses and dogs who lived on farms, or in the wild. Sometimes he rented videos about collies or Dalmatians for the family to watch together. These were movies about Lassie and Pongo and Perdita—dogs everybody in the world seemed to love. Except Sara. Each time her father put a tape in the machine, Sara waited until the lights were turned down low and then tiptoed out of the room. She didn't know which was worse: being afraid of dogs, or her parents always trying to make her not afraid.

Sara knew that Will thought she was a baby and a scaredy-cat. But if he called her these names out loud, Mrs. Barker would scrunch her eyebrows at him and say, "Everyone's afraid of something." And Mr. Barker would say, "That's enough, William," in his sternest voice.

Sara's grandparents and aunts and uncles never said anything to her about dogs. On occasion, though, one of them might whisper to her mother or father, "Is she still afraid of *you-know-whats*?"

Sara especially didn't want her friends to know about this. Through the years she had come up with lots of tricks to keep them from finding out.

If she and Cindy and Jessica were walking along one side of the street and saw a dog headed toward them, even a dog on a leash, Sara always came up with an excuse to make an escape. "Let's chase butterflies," or "Let's see if somebody with a hole in her pocket dropped money on the sidewalk around the corner," or "Let's look under that giant rock at the other end of the block in case fairies maybe really live there." Then she would let out a whoop and lead the way

across the street or down an alley or through the backyard of a nearby house.

When Susie or Margaret or Jane invited her over, Sara would casually say, "Well, you do have a dog, and I'm sort of allergic." Then she would make pretend sneezes and scratch at an invisible rash. Susie or Margaret or Jane would say, "That's okay, because if you come I promise we'll keep the dog down in the basement." This worked for daytime visits, but Sara would never go for a sleepover to a house where there was a dog. That's because she was sure that sometime, during the night, the dog would sneak out of the basement and come and find her. Even in the dark.

It seemed to Sara that all her other

friends, those who didn't have dogs, had pictures of dogs. Big posters of golden retrievers or German shepherds or Labs looked down at her from the walls of their bedrooms. Stuffed Scotties or poodles or beagles perched on their beds.

And, even though Sara knew it was the silliest thing of all, she didn't like these unreal dogs either. Just looking at them made her feel cold and clammy all over, almost the way the real ones did.

And it's all Aunt Lillibet's fault, she thought.

Fred

Aunt Lillibet was Mr. Barker's great-aunt, which made her Sara's great-great-aunt. She lived in Virginia in a one-story lavender house that had a sloping backyard with a stream at the very bottom.

Aunt Lillibet sent books to the children for Christmas and their birthdays. She wrote letters and drew tiny pictures where some of the words should have been. Houses and stars and snowmen decorated the pages, along with owls and picket fences. Mr. and Mrs. Barker sent books to Aunt Lillibet for Christmas and *her* birthday. They also sent pictures of Will and Sara playing in the snow or at the beach or dressed in their Halloween costumes.

In spite of the presents and the letters and the pictures, the children had never actually met Aunt Lillibet until the spring after Sara's fourth birthday, when the family went to visit her for a weekend. All the way down in the car, Mr. Barker had told stories about Aunt Lillibet: how she taught him to fly a kite when he was little, and how to catch crabs with chicken necks as bait, tied to a piece of string. He described his aunt as a tall, imposing woman with heaps of white hair piled up on her head, all held in place by thin yellow sticks that looked like knitting needles, or maybe pencils. He said that when she spoke, her voice made a scratchy, sandpaper-on-wood kind of sound, and that, to his way of thinking, she always smelled like cinnamon toast.

"And," Mr. Barker went on, "while she wouldn't give a cat the time of day, Aunt Lillibet *loves* dogs."

• When Mr. Barker stopped the car in the driveway of the lavender house, Aunt Lillibet was in the front yard piling mulch around the azalea bushes. As soon as she saw the car, she threw her trowel up in the air, peeled off her gardening gloves, and hurried across the lawn. "You're here," Aunt Lillibet said in her sandpaper voice as they all piled out of the car. "You're actually *here*.

"Just look at you—look at you," said Aunt Lillibet, first to Mr. Barker, then to Mrs. Barker, and then to Will and Sara. "Come in—come in. We've been waiting for you. I told Fred you were coming and he's so excited . . ."

Aunt Lillibet shooed them all through the front door and into the hall, and before Sara had a chance to ask who Fred was, she heard a scritch-scratching on the floorboards. She heard panting and snorting and yelping, and suddenly a huge yellow dog came bounding through the dining room, heading straight toward them.

"Look, Fred, they're here," trilled Aunt Lillibet. "I told you they would be, and they are."

But Fred kept on running, past Mr. Barker and Mrs. Barker, and even Will. He spun around, skidded on the scatter rug, and put his giant paws on Sara's shoulders, pushing her down, down, down onto the floor.

"Fred, sit, *sit*, and show some manners," called Aunt Lillibet.

Sara screamed. She started to cry, with big gulping sobs and little squeals mixed in.

Fred wagged his tail. He showed his

pointy white teeth and licked Sara's face with his long red tongue.

Sara felt the warm, wet slobber. She saw his dark eyes looking down at her. She screamed again.

"He's only trying to say hello," Aunt Lillibet said, clapping her hands. "Here, Freddie. Here, doggie."

But Fred gave Sara's face an even bigger lick. He breathed his hot breath on her neck and did a kind of dance with his giant yellow paws.

Sara screamed her loudest scream ever. She saw her mother and brother and Aunt Lillibet looking at her. She saw her aunt pull the huge animal away from her and felt her father scoop her up in his arms almost at the same time. "There, there," Mr. Barker said. "It's all right now."

"Poor baby," said Mrs. Barker, patting her on the back. "That was scary, I know. But you're okay."

"He didn't bite her or anything," said Will, but even he reached out and gave Sara a friendly poke on the shoulder.

"Fred's sorry," said Aunt Lillibet, brushing the hair out of Sara's eyes. "Fred says he only wanted to play." And with her other hand she scratched the dog behind his left ear.

Sara looked all around. She looked down at the dog now sitting quietly at Aunt Lillibet's side. Then she buried her face in her father's shoulder and said, "I don't *like* dogs. I don't like dogs *forever*."

During the rest of the visit, Aunt Lillibet kept Fred outside when Sara was inside, and inside when Sara was out. Even when they all went out for a walk, though, or to the ice cream store, Sara thought about Fred and how he was back at the house waiting for her. And every time she closed her eyes, she saw his giant paws and his pointy teeth and could almost feel his hot dog breath against her neck.

It was after her visit to Aunt Lillibet and Fred that Sara began to insist on crossing to the other side of the street if she saw a dog coming toward her. It was after the visit that just seeing a picture of a dog began to make her feel clammy and cold all over.

It was from that time on that Sara began saying, either out loud or just under her breath, "I *really* don't like dogs forever."

Who Is Harrington?

When Mr. Willis, who lived next door to Sara's family, decided to move to an apartment, he put a blue-and-white FOR SALE sign in his front yard and pots of red geraniums on the porch steps. He washed the windows and cut the grass that didn't quite need cutting yet and even edged along the sidewalk with an electric edger he borrowed from Mr. Barker.

One afternoon Sara sat on her porch and watched as Mr. Willis snip-snip-snipped at his bushes, turning them into fat round green balls. It gave her a weird-all-over feeling that the fact that he was moving away didn't make her even a little bit sad, especially since he'd lived there for as long as she could remember. He's all right, Sara thought, and always says "Good morning" or "Good afternoon." But that's *all* he says, never anything else, like "Is that a new bike?" or "How was your Christmas?" Besides, every Halloween he turns out all the lights in his house, gets in his car, and drives away—and doesn't come back till the trick-or-treaters are home in bed.

"Kids would be nice," said Sara, as she and her mother stood at their window on a Saturday morning and watched a man and woman go in to look at Mr. Willis's house. "A girl for me and a boy for Will. Or maybe only a girl, just my age, and then she could hang around with Cindy, Jessica, and me. Or even a baby'd be okay and then when I got older I could babysit it."

"Kids *would* be nice," agreed Mrs. Barker. "We'll keep our fingers crossed."

Over the next six weeks Sara watched old people and young people, one-at-a-time people and entire groups go in and out of the house next door. And then one day, when she and Will came home from school, there was a red board attached to the FOR SALE sign, with the word SOLD in big white letters.

"Who *bought* it?" Sara asked.

"Bought what?" asked Will.

"The house. Look!"

Will shrugged and fished in his pocket for the key to unlock the door. "Somebody, I guess," he said.

"Yeah, but, somebody *who*?" said Sara as she dropped her backpack on the table and went to stand at the front window. She pressed her nose against the glass and stared at the sign, dreaming of the children who just might be moving in.

"I see the house sold," said Mrs. Barker when she came in from the school where she taught kindergarten.

"I see the house sold," said Mr. Barker when he came in from his job at the cable company.

"Yes, but who *to*?" said Sara. "I really need to know."

"Don't worry," her mother said. "We'll find out soon enough. Next time we see Mr. Willis, we'll just ask. Okay?"

But the trouble was, Mr. Willis seemed to have become invisible. When everybody in the Barker family left in the morning, he was still in his house. When the Barkers came home, Mr. Willis was still at work. They didn't see him picking up his newspaper in the morning or getting his mail or watering his geraniums. They didn't see him sweeping the sidewalk or carrying in groceries from the store.

Then finally, a week and a half after the SOLD sign had gone up, Sara and her mother were out front one day just as Mr. Willis was getting into his car.

"Oh, Mr. Willis," Mrs. Barker called, "we've all been wondering who bought your house."

"Harrington. The name is Harrington," said Mr. Willis, and he started his engine and drove away.

A New Neighbor

*M*r. Harrington?
  Mrs. Harrington?
  Big or little kid Harringtons?
  Sara had fretted about these things ever since Mr. Willis told them the name of the person who'd bought his house. But Mr.

Willis never told them any more than that, and then one day he finally moved away.

"It's not fair," Sara said, as the moving van with all Mr. Willis's belongings in it pulled out from the curb. "He could've told us who was moving in next door. I mean, are there kids, and how many, and how old. All the really important stuff."

"So now it's the myyyysssssterrry family," said Will, stretching the word *mystery* out in his creepiest voice. "The myyyysssssterrry Harringtons, and maybe they're really vampires or ghouls or monsters, and Mr. Willis knew it and didn't want us to find out, and that's why he—"

"That's enough, Will," said Mrs. Barker.

"I'm sure they're perfectly nice people, whoever they are, and we'll meet them soon enough."

Soon enough wasn't really soon enough for Sara, and she began to watch for clues.

One afternoon, when she came home from school, there was a blue car with flower decals along one side parked in front of the house next door. There were lights on in the cellar and in the garage, and Sara settled down on her own front porch to watch. She watched and she watched, until finally the phone rang and she had to run inside to answer it. When she came back, the lights were out and the car was gone.

Another time, Sara saw a painter pull up

in front of the house. While he was busy unloading his ladders and drop cloths and buckets of paint, she ran over to talk to him. "Hi," she said. "I live next door, and I wondered if you know who's moving in here."

"Harrington," the painter said, as he picked up his ladder and headed for the steps.

A week after Mr. Willis moved out, Sara, Cindy, and Jessica were sitting on the Barkers' front steps eating peanut butter crackers and staring at the empty house. "Look! There's Mr. Miller, the mailman," said Cindy, brushing crumbs off her knees.

"So what's the big deal?" said Sara. "He comes every day."

"Don't you get it?" said Cindy. "He comes every day and leaves mail in all the boxes, so he has to know who it's *for*, and—"

"We'll just ask him," said Jessica, spraying cracker crumbs as she spoke. "I mean, the letters would at least say stuff like *Mr.* Harringon or *Mrs.* Harrington, but maybe if there are party invitations or birthday cards, they'll have kid names, too."

The girls watched Mr. Miller work his way up one side of the street and down the other. When he got to the Barkers' house, he handed Sara four letters and a magazine. "And how are you ladies this afternoon?" he said.

"O-kay, I guess," said Cindy, in her most forlorn voice.

"Only okay?" asked Mr. Miller. "Seems you three ought to be able to come up with something better than okay."

"It's just that we have a problem," said Jessica, in *her* most forlorn voice.

"On account of we really need to know who's moving in next door and if there're kids and all, so we thought maybe you could look and tell us what names are on the letters you have for them. Pleeease," begged Sara.

Mr. Miller laughed. He reached in his bag and pulled out a letter for the house next door. "Sorry, ladies," he said, shaking his head and turning the letter so they could see it. "All it says is 'Resident.'"

.   .   .

On a Saturday morning two weeks after Mr. Willis left, Sara glanced out of an upstairs window in time to see a green-and-yellow moving van pull up in front of the house next door. The blue car with the flower decals parked in back of it, and a tall string bean of a woman got out. Sara caught her breath, and pressed her forehead against the windowpane, as her mother walked across the lawn and held out her hand to the woman. She watched the two of them for a while, then turned and raced down the stairs.

"Well, the mystery is solved," said Mrs. Barker, coming in the front door just as Sara was heading out. "That is Ms. Harrington— Ms. Barbara Harrington. She lives alone, and—"

Sara groaned.

Her mother reached out and pulled her close. "I know you're disappointed, Sara," she said. "But I'm sure Ms. Harrington will be a fine neighbor."

Next-Door Dogs?

"**A** fine neighbor?" Sara repeated what her mother had said, only this time with a question mark at the end. She sighed, thinking how Ms. Harrington probably *would* be a fine neighbor, the same way Mr. Willis had been a fine neighbor. That she would probably say "Good morning" and

"Good afternoon" but never, never ask what book Sara was reading or what she and Cindy and Jessica planned to do on their summer vacations. She wondered if this new neighbor even liked Halloween.

"But there aren't any children moving in there with her." Sara sighed again and went off to the kitchen to call Cindy and Jessica and tell them the news. Or, rather, the non-news.

At Cindy's house, the phone rang and rang. Not even the answering machine picked up.

At Jessica's house, her mother said that Jessica had gone downtown to the aquarium with her grandparents.

After she hung up, Sara sighed her biggest sigh ever. And because she couldn't think of anything else to do, she took her book and slumped into a wicker chair on the front porch to watch the moving men next door.

She watched them carry in beds and chairs and bookcases. She saw them balance rugs rolled up like long sausages on their shoulders and struggle up the front steps with a red-and-blue-striped sofa. She saw a desk and a dining room table and about a million boxes disappear through the front door.

After a while Will came out and sat across from her. "So, what'd you learn about the mysterious Ms. Harrington?" he asked.

"Bo-ring," said Sara. "It's just a bunch of beds and chairs and lamps and stuff." With that she slid down lower in her chair, picked up her book, and started to read.

She had just come to the end of a chapter when she heard Will say a loud *"Wow"* followed by an even louder "DOGHOUSE."

She looked up just in time to see one of the movers coming down the ramp from the truck carrying a large green doghouse. He set it on the ground, went back into the truck, and came out a few minutes later carrying a large *red* doghouse.

"TWO DOGHOUSES," shouted Will. "Scaredy-cat Sara's going to have two dogs living right next door."

"Stop it, Will," said Sara, pulling her feet up and tucking them under her. "Just stop it."

But Will didn't pay any attention. He dropped down onto all fours, pretending to be a dog. He wagged his back end and reached out to Sara with his make-believe paws. He growled and barked and growled some more. "I'm a dog," said Will in his gruffest, most doglike voice. "I'm *two* dogs, and I'm worse than all the vampires and ghouls and monsters in the world—and I'm moving in next door. And because of that, Sara won't ever be able to sit on the porch again. And every time the family eats out back, someone will have to hand food in the screen door to baby Sara."

"*William,*" called Mr. Barker in his sternest voice, from just inside the screen door. "Come in here right now."

After Will left, Sara put her feet on the floor again. She leaned forward and rested her chin on the porch railing. Her stomach felt quivery way down deep. Her hands were cold and clammy, and her knees shook. She wanted to run and hide, but her body seemed to be made of stone. She was stuck there, watching the movers carry first one doghouse and then the other around to Ms. Harrington's backyard.

Suddenly Sara jumped up, as if invisible puppet strings had yanked at her. She raced through the house to the back porch and crouched down so that only a bit of her head showed over the railing.

Ms. Harrington was standing in the middle of Mr. Willis's yard, which was now her yard. "Maybe," she said, her voice drifting over the fence like the sound of a bell, "we should put the green one under the maple tree and the red one next to the rose of Sharon." She waved one hand in the direction of the moving men and added, "Unless we should make it just the opposite. Or maybe both side by side." She squinted and stepped back. "Or facing each other, so that way—"

Just then she looked over and saw the top of Sara's head above the railing. "Hel-looooo," she called. "Would you come and give me a bit of advice?"

Sara inched her head higher. She stood

up slowly and made her way to the steps, holding tight to the banister. "You mean me?" she said in her croakiest voice.

"Of course I mean you," the woman said. "I'm Barbara Harrington—and you are . . . ?"

"Sara. Barker," Sara said, clutching the railing even tighter.

"Well, Sara Barker, I'm trying to decide just where to put my dogs' houses. Here, or maybe there—though I don't know why I worry because they're both more apt to settle themselves comfortably at either end of the living room couch."

"Dogs?" said Sara in a small, squeaky voice. "You have *dogs*? We're going to have next-door dogs?"

About Max and Jake

"Two dogs," said Ms. Harrington, moving over to the fence and resting her arms on top. "Two wonderful, spectacular, and amazingly intelligent dogs."

Up close, Sara thought Ms. Harrington was fierce-looking, with gray-brown hair, shaggy eyebrows, sticking-out cheekbones, and a beak for a nose. But when she smiled—a great, wide smile—her face suddenly turned soft, like a worn and crinkly cushion. "Well," she said, "at least *I* think they're wonderful and spectacular, but I know for a fact that they're intelligent."

Sara looked at the red and green doghouses, which seemed to be getting larger by the minute. "*Big* dogs?" she squeaked.

"Good-size," said the woman. "I like a dog with enough heft to him so I know there's something at the other end of the leash."

Sara swallowed hard. "*Young* dogs?" she asked.

"Well, they're not puppies, but they're not senior citizens, either," said Ms. Harring-

ton. "Max, the yellow Lab, is two, and Jake, the Dalmatian, is three."

Sara thought that two and three sounded very young indeed. She closed her eyes and pictured two frisky, rambunctious dogs leaping at the fence between her yard and the one next door. Maybe even sailing over the top.

"*Barking* dogs?" she wanted to know next.

"Well, now that could be a problem," said Ms. Harrington. "We had a long talk when we bought the house, Max and Jake and I, and I did my best to explain that excessive barking might not endear them to the neighbors. They said they'd try, but what with a new mailman and a whole bunch of unfamiliar sounds and smells . . ." She shook her head and added, "I hope you and your family will be a little patient with them. At least in the beginning."

"I don't hear them *now*," said Sara, inching closer to the edge of the porch and looking in all the corners of the yard.

"Oh, that's because they're at the kennel. I thought it best to board them during the move, but I'll pick them up tomorrow. I know they'll both take to you right away."

With that Sara took a giant step backward, pulled open the screen door, and stood behind it. She held tight to the doorframe for a minute, trying to decide if it would be rude for her to keep going, right into the kitchen. Without even saying goodbye to the new neighbor.

Before Sara could decide, Ms. Harrington called out to her. "But now I'd like to know some more about you. Things I don't already know."

With that Sara came out from behind the screen door and peered down at the woman. "But that'd be *everything* on account of you can't already know *anything* about me—because we've only just met," she said.

"Oh, but I do," Ms. Harrington said. "I know your name is Sara Barker—you told me that. I know you're tall, and thin, what I'd call lanky, and look like you play soccer."

Sara nodded.

"I know you're ten, or maybe eleven."

"Nine," said Sara.

"Okay, but a very grownup nine. And I

know you have a mop of wonderfully curly dark hair, and, I'm guessing here, but I'll bet anything you like to read."

Sara nodded again.

"Probably adventure stories, and maybe fantasy. Am I right?"

Sara grinned and shook her head. "Nuh-uh," she said. "I mostly like mysteries and books about kids like me."

"Ah," said Ms. Harrington. "Good choices. I like a good mystery, and I'd *love* to find a book about a scarecrow of a woman with two great dogs who just moved into a brown shingle house on McHale Street." She stopped and looked up at the sky a minute before saying, "But back to the subject at hand—I know you don't like dogs very much."

"You *do?*" said Sara, inching closer to the porch railing.

"And that you might even be a little afraid of them," the neighbor went on.

"You know that, too?" asked Sara. "But how—my mother wouldn't ever—or my father either—"

Ms. Harrington shook her head. "No, nothing like that. I just know, that's all. Call it a hunch. But that's okay, not liking dogs, I mean. And even being a little afraid. Why, I myself am not at all fond of spiders."

"But what about . . ." Sara waved her hand in the direction of the red and green doghouses. "What about them?"

"Max and Jake? Remember when I told you that they were amazingly intelligent dogs? Well, they're *so* amazingly intelligent that I can promise you, once I explain how you feel, they'll never go on your side of the fence, and never ever lick and slobber on you—if you don't want to be licked and slobbered on."

Before Sara could decide what to say to that, Ms. Harrington went on, "And if I ever get my boxes unpacked and the yard taken care of and my pictures hung, and if I ever find time to make cookies again, well—I'll just deliver them to you out front. Okay?"

"Okay," said Sara, who was beginning to think that, just maybe, Ms. Harrington might be more than a fine neighbor after all.

Cookies and Jump Rope

The next morning Ms. Harrington picked Max and Jake up at the kennel and brought them home to their new house. Sara was reading on her front porch when they arrived, and as soon as she saw the dogs tumbling out of the car, she put her book down and went inside. Just to be on the safe side.

A few minutes later, as Sara was watching from the kitchen window, Ms. Harrington opened her back door and the dogs ran out into the yard. They sniffed at the grass and trees and shrubs, and even at the yellow flowerpot at the end of the walk. They nosed at the green and red doghouses and played some kind of game where they went in and out the little doors in front, over and over again.

They raced in giant circles around the yard. Sara thought that sometimes Max seemed to be chasing Jake, and sometimes Jake seemed to be chasing Max.

She saw them jump at the fence between the houses, and then head up onto Ms. Harrington's back porch and scratch at the door.

And Sara heard them bark. Max had a deep, rolling, anything-goes kind of bark. But Jake's was sharper and bossier, as if he was saying, "I want to come in *now*."

Even though the dogs were outside and in their very own yard, Sara had a cold, quivery feeling in the middle of her stomach. And she found herself holding tight to the kitchen windowsill. Just in case.

Sometimes Ms. Harrington took Max and Jake for walks. If Sara was sitting on her front porch when they went out, she always waved. Ms. Harrington waved back, but she never expected Sara to come and meet the dogs.

If Sara and Cindy and Jessica were running through the neighborhood and saw Ms. Harrington and her dogs coming toward them, Sara always went in search of lost coins or fairies living under rocks. Then she would wave and call "Hi, Ms. Harrington," in her bravest voice. From the other side of the street.

Sara, Jessica, Cindy, and Cindy's three cousins from Virginia were all outside playing a game of sardines one day. It was Jessica's turn to hide, while the others counted to one hundred by twos. Then the other girls set out on their own to find her and sneak into her hiding place. Sara looked behind the trellis on the Hendersons' lawn and alongside of the Ramoses' garage. She raced through the clump of bushes in Jessica's front yard and swung around the corner. And suddenly she was face-to-face with Ms. Harrington and Max and Jake.

Sara was so close she could feel their dog breath on her skin. She could hear the swish-swish-swish of their tails, and when Jake opened his mouth, she could see the tip of his long red tongue. But it was as if her feet were stuck onto the sidewalk and she couldn't move.

Ms. Harrington yanked sharply on the leashes. She said, "Max! Jake! Sit."

The dogs sat, and Sara's feet were suddenly unstuck. She waved a small, quick

wave to Ms. Harrington, then turned and ran as fast as she could. In the other direction.

Even though Sara had met Max and Jake face-to-face, whenever her mother asked her to take the trash to the garbage can in the backyard, she was still careful to look out the window first. She had to make sure that Max and Jake were safely in their own house. And even then, she hurried both ways.

One day, not long after school let out for the summer, Sara, Cindy, and Jessica were sitting on the Barkers' front steps trying to decide what to do.

"Helloooooo," they heard, and looked up to see Ms. Harrington cutting across the front lawn. She had a blue plastic bag slung over one arm and was carrying a plate covered with aluminum foil in her other hand. "I was just in a cookie mood, but I can't possibly eat the whole batch, so I thought you girls might help me out."

"Mmmmmmmmmm," Cindy and Jessica said.

"Mmmmmmmmmm," said Sara, even before she remembered to introduce Ms. Harrington to her friends.

"I've seen you girls with Sara from time to time, but we just haven't properly met," said Ms. Harrington, settling onto the third step from the bottom. She pulled a bottle of apple juice and four paper cups out of her bag and whisked the cover off the plate of cookies.

"Double mmmmmm," said Jessica.

"Triple mmmmmm," said Sara.

"Double, triple, quadruple mmmmm-mmm," said Cindy, reaching for a cookie.

While they ate, they talked: about the camp Cindy was going to, and Jessica's birthday party, and the trip the Barkers were taking to the beach later in the summer. Ms. Harrington told them about her nieces and nephews who lived close by, and about their children, her great-nieces and great-nephews who would be coming often to visit. And afterward, when the cookies were gone and the trash was all cleaned up,

Ms. Harrington offered to turn one end of Cindy's jump rope.

"I don't jump too fast anymore," she said, "but I can turn forever."

Later that afternoon, when the girls were playing Monopoly at Jessica's house, Cindy turned to Sara and said, "I think your new neighbor is cool."

"Way cool," said Sara, all the while thinking, *If only she didn't have those dogs.*

What the Dogs Were Saying

Sometimes Ms. Harrington made cookies for the girls. Sometimes she made
brownies, or even blondies. Sometimes she
turned one end of the jump rope, or played
card games on the Barkers' front steps.

And sometimes her great-nieces and
great-nephews came for a visit to play in the

backyard with Max and Jake, or to go with Ms. Harrington when she took the dogs for a walk.

During these visits, though Ms. Harrington told her she was always welcome, Sara would just stand at the window, watching. At these times she felt a little bit sad and a little bit lonely, and not nearly as brave as she wanted to be.

One Saturday morning early in July, Sara was in the kitchen eating breakfast. Her father and Will had gone off to the hardware store. Her mother, who had just come in from running, was upstairs in the shower.

Just as Sara was chasing the last Cheerio

around her bowl, she heard a storm of barking coming from the yard next door. There was Max's deep, rolling bark, louder than it had ever been before. And there was Jake's sharp and bossy bark, which seemed to be saying, "Do something—and do it now, now, now."

Sara got up and went out onto the porch, where she was sure the sound of barking would swallow her up. *Ruff ruff ruff yap yap ruff yap ruff.* Then there was a sudden silence when, Sara thought, both dogs must have stopped to catch their breath so they could bark again.

And in that silence, Sara heard a thin and wavery voice calling, "Somebody—

somebody—I need help—I need help now . . ."

"Ms. Harrington? Is that you? Is something wrong?" Sara called, but by then Max and Jake were barking again—*ruff ruff yap yap ruff*—and prancing around the steps of the house next door.

Sara ran inside and up the stairs. "Mom!" she called, banging on the bathroom door, then opening it, gasping at the steam from the shower. "Mom, there's something wrong next door and the dogs are barking like crazy and somebody called *help* and I think it's Ms. Harrington and you'd better come right now."

Mrs. Barker turned off the water and stuck her head out from behind the shower curtain. "What did you hear, Sara? What did Ms. Harrington say?"

" '*I need help*,' that's what she said, except her voice was all wobbly, but it sounded like Ms. Harrington's, only then the dogs started barking again and—"

"Okay," said Mrs. Barker. "I'm going to rinse this soap out of my hair and throw on some clothes, and then I'll be right there. But you go on down and over to Ms. Harrington's and see what you can do. And tell her I'm on my way."

Sara turned and ran down the steps and out onto the back porch, where the sound of barking was even fiercer than before. Suddenly she stopped. "Me? Over there?" she said out loud.

Her knees shook. Her hands felt clammy. There was a cold, quivery feeling in the bottom of her stomach.

The dogs kept barking while Sara forced herself to look at them: at their gigantic mouths and pointy teeth and humongous paws. And as she watched, she saw them run over to the fence between the yards and then back to the figure lying on the ground at the foot of the steps.

Sara to the Rescue

The dogs stopped barking as soon as Sara scrambled over the fence and dropped into the yard next door. They turned to look at her, Max cocking his head to one side, and Jake to the other. They wagged their tails, and Max scratched at the ground next to Ms. Harrington as if to say, "Get over here and *do* something."

Then they started barking again. They raced toward Sara and ran in circles around her. Round and round and round. Her knees started to shake and she had a quivery feeling in her stomach until she remembered what Ms. Harrington had done the day Sara and her friends were playing sardines.

Sara drew herself up tall, just as Ms. Harrington had done. She said "SIT" in her biggest voice, just as Ms. Harrington had done. But the dogs kept on running in circles around her, almost as if they were pushing her along.

"Oh, I'm so glad to see someone, but

could you come closer?" called Ms. Harrington, her voice still wavery. "I was afraid that with all that barking no one would ever hear me, though I'm sure Max and Jake were sending their own kind of message."

"But what happened?" asked Sara, pushing her way through the dogs and moving close to the woman. She looked down at Ms. Harrington and saw the way her right leg seemed to be twisted in a very un-leg-like way. "What'd you do?"

"Something very silly, I'm afraid. I was coming out with my new blue flowerpot, a watering can full of water, the cushions for the chaise, and the morning paper, and I couldn't really see where I was going and seem to have stepped where there was no step."

For the first time, Sara noticed bits of blue pottery and splatters of water on the ground around Ms. Harrington. The chaise cushions were all in a heap. In their excitement, Max and Jake had trampled the newspaper to shreds.

"My mom's on her way, soon as she gets the soap out of her hair and puts clothes on, but what do you need for me to do?"

"I think what I probably need is for someone to come and get me and take me off to have something done to this leg, which at the moment feels like a steamroller's going back and forth over it. The phone is on the wall in the kitchen, and if you could just go inside and call 911 and give them the address and . . . whatever . . ." Ms. Harrington's voice was suddenly thin and raggedy. There was a film of sweat on her face.

"Okay," said Sara. "I'll go, and then I'll be right back." Without thinking, she shoved Jake out of the way and ran up the steps and into the kitchen. She found the phone on the wall over a giant dog bed that, Sara was sure, was large enough for both Jake and Max. She picked up the receiver, stared at it for a second, took a deep breath, and pushed 9-1-1.

The woman who answered the phone asked her name and the telephone number

she was calling from. "My name is Sara Barker and I live at 146 McHale Street and I'm calling from next door at 144, only I don't know the phone number on account of it's Ms. Harrington's house and she's outside at the bottom of the steps with her leg all twisted and funny, and she thinks somebody at 911 should come."

"Okay, Sara," the woman said. "And are you there alone with Ms. Harrington?"

"Yes, except my mom's coming once she gets the soap out of her hair. And then there're the dogs, and that's how I knew about Ms. Harrington being hurt. Because of the barking."

"All right, Sara. You've done a good job, and we'll have an ambulance there in just a few minutes. Meanwhile, you go back and tell Ms. Harrington that help is on the way."

When Sara went back outside, her mother was kneeling on the ground next to Ms. Harrington.

"They're coming," said Sara, clearing away broken pieces of pottery and sitting on the ground. "The 911 lady said to tell you they're sending an ambulance and they'll be here soon."

"Thank you," Ms. Harrington said, reaching for Sara's hand. "Thank you."

"I'm going along in the ambulance with you," said Mrs. Barker. "My husband will be home any minute, and Sara can just run up to Jessica's until he gets here."

Ms. Harrington shook her head, then winced, as if moving her head somehow hurt her twisted leg. "No, no," she said. "I'm a tough old bird, and I'll be just fine. Want you here with Sara, and if you wouldn't mind, I need for you to call my niece Linda and ask her to come see to the dogs, maybe even take them to her place. Till I'm home again." She closed her eyes and whispered, "Linda's number is on the yellow pad over the phone in the kitchen." With that she dropped her head back, and her breath seemed to be coming in little puffs.

Max and Jake heard the ambulance before anyone else. Their ears pricked up. They started to run back and forth along the fence to the front yard. And then they started to bark, a deep rolling bark for Max, and a sharper, it's-about-time bark for Jake. Ms. Harrington opened her eyes and winked at Sara while squeezing her hand.

It wasn't until after the ambulance had taken Ms. Harrington to the hospital and Linda had come by to pick up Max and Jake that Sara had time to think about all that had happened that morning. She hoped Ms. Harrington's leg wasn't too bad and that she'd be home soon.

It wasn't until after all this that she let herself think about the dogs and how they had barked and barked until someone came to help. And then she thought how, even when she went into the next-door yard, they hadn't licked her with their slobbery tongues or bitten her with their pointy teeth, or pushed her down, down, down with their giant paws.

That night for dessert the Barkers had cookie crumb ice cream with swirls of whipped cream on top. "For Sara, because of what she did," said Mrs. Barker as she put the bowls on the table.

"And *we* have a Sara song," her father said, as he and Will got up and stood at the end of the table. "It's to the tune of 'Twinkle, Twinkle, Little Star.'" And when they sang, Mr. Barker's voice was loud and clear, while Will's shook with laughter.

"*Sara Barker saves the day,*

Calming dogs along the way.

Bravely calling 911

To get help for Ms. Harrington . . ."

Afterward Sara's dad kissed her on the forehead. Her brother gave her a high five. And barked.

A Very Quiet House Next Door

Ms. Harrington spent three nights in the hospital. On the second day, Mrs. Barker went to visit her, and when she got back, she told the rest of the family that their neighbor was doing well. "The doctor set her broken leg, the nurses are giving her all kinds of attention, and just as soon as the physical therapist makes sure she can handle her crutches and get in and out of a car with that big clunky cast, she'll be home."

"Then Cindy and Jessica and I can go to see her?" said Sara.

"Once she's home—she's counting on it," her mother said. "Meanwhile, Sara, it's a wonder your ears weren't burning this afternoon, the way Ms. Harrington was going on."

"My *ears*?" said Sara. "What's wrong with my ears?"

"There's nothing *wrong* with them," said Mrs. Barker. "But you know how they say that if someone is talking about you, your ears will burn."

"Yeah, but . . ." Sara rubbed her ears and looked at her mother.

"It's an old wives' tale, or something," said her mother. "I just meant that Ms. Harrington is regaling everyone who will listen—doctors, nurses, aides, her roommate, and even her roommate's visitors—with stories of how her neighbor Sara Barker came to her rescue. How you heard her dogs barking and knew something was wrong, and then you heard her calling for help and came right over that fence and took care of things. Even though you're not really especially fond of dogs."

Sara stood a little taller while her mother was telling her this. And she thought that maybe her ears *had* burned a little this afternoon, just about the time her mother was visiting at the hospital.

. . .

While she was laid up in the hospital, Ms. Harrington's dogs stayed with Linda. Sara remembered watching from her front porch when Linda came to pick them up, and seeing Max and Jake climb into the back of the van with Ms. Harrington's great-nieces and great-nephews.

Sara had seen the van head down the street and around the corner. After that, it was strangely quiet in the yard next door. There were no deep, rolling barks, and no sharp, bossy ones either. There was no yelping at the fence or scratching at Ms. Harrington's back door.

And at night Ms. Harrington's house was

dark from top to bottom. Even the lantern-shaped light by the front walkway.

Sara felt a huge ache right in the middle of her body that came, she was sure, from missing Ms. Harrington.

She felt a tiny surprise twinge, also, that just might have come from missing Max and Jake.

Welcome Home

The day after Ms. Harrington came home from the hospital, Sara, Cindy, and Jessica met at Cindy's house to bake a cake. Cindy's mother turned the oven on and made sure the square cake pan was well greased. Then Jessica added the eggs and water to the cake mix, while Sara and Cindy took turns stirring the batter.

Once the cake was done and had had a chance to cool, the girls frosted it with chocolate icing. They put yellow icing squiggles around the edges. Then, very carefully, Jessica wrote WELCOME, Cindy wrote HOME, and Sara wrote MS. H. across the top in the same yellow icing.

The girls took the cake, a handful of paper napkins, and four cans of soda and went down the street to Ms. Harrington's house.

"D'you think she'll be surprised?" asked Cindy.

"Yeah," said Sara. "Unless my mother told. She was over there this morning."

"She wouldn't have. Told about the cake, I mean. Anyway, *I* think she'll be surprised," said Jessica as they went up the steps to the house. "Come on, let's ring."

They had scarcely touched the doorbell when they heard a sudden burst of barking coming from inside the house. This was followed by the scritch-scratch sound of toenails on hardwood floors as Max suddenly appeared at one of the little windows next to the front door, and Jake at the other.

"Hey, the dogs are back," said Cindy.

"Way cool," said Jessica. "I was hoping they would be."

Sara held tight to the cake plate, willing herself not to drop it. Her knees felt wobbly and she was cold all over, as she wondered when the dogs had gotten home. Suddenly she had a long-ago memory of Aunt Lillibet and Fred, and when she looked at Max and Jake through the windows, their teeth seemed pointier than ever. And they were slobbering all over the glass.

I can't go in, she thought.

You can't not *go in,* a little voice from deep inside of her answered. *Besides, you did before. The day Ms. Harrington fell.*

That was different, Sara argued. I didn't have a choice.

You don't have one now, the voice said. *What with Ms. Harrington expecting you to come for a visit. And if you turn and run, Cindy and Jessica will know you're afraid.*

I'm *not* afraid. Not exactly, anyway.

Then, of course, there's the story of Ms. Harrington telling everyone in the entire hospital how incredibly brave you were . . . The voice began to fade and drift away.

Sara took a deep breath. She stiffened her legs. She straightened her backbone. Then she stared in at Max and Jake, who somehow didn't seem fierce or slobbery anymore, and almost looked as if they were smiling at her.

"Yeah," Sara said. "That's cool about the dogs being back."

Once the girls were inside the house, Max and Jake crowded around them. They nuzzled their feet and made sniffing noises when Cindy and Jessica scratched them on the ears. Then they lifted their heads, higher and higher, sniffing the air as if they smelled chocolate cake with yellow icing squiggles on the top.

Ms. Harrington led the way into the kitchen, bump-bump-bumping along on her crutches. She settled herself at the table and pointed to the cupboard over the sink, where the plates were kept.

"That is a handsome cake," she said, a grin spreading across her face. "And looks almost too good to eat—*except* hospital food isn't much, and I'm *hungry*. How about you girls?"

"Starving."

"Really starving."

"Really, really incredibly starving."

After that, Cindy opened the sodas and put one in front of each place. Jessica handed out plates, forks, and paper napkins, and Sara cut the cake, making sure to give Ms. Harrington the largest piece.

While Ms. Harrington and the girls were eating, the dogs made themselves comfortable under the table. Sara heard the thump of their tails against the floor. She heard them sigh from time to time and make other snuffly, snorty sounds. After a bit, Jake put his head down on Sara's foot and went to sleep.

And Sara didn't mind at all.